PAWS OFF

EMMA BRAY

CHAPTER 1

Stone

I READJUST the box in my arms and take a deep breath of the salty sea air.

Yeah, I think this move is going to do me good.

I grew up in New York City as an only child. My parents were great and doted on me, but they're not here anymore. I finally realized nothing was keeping me in that God-forsaken place, so I took the jump and moved to sunny California to be near my best friend.

I met Jeremy at college. We were thrown together as roommates, and we just hit it off and became total bros. Oh, we're as different as night and day. But maybe we complement each other or something because we get along so well.

However, when Jeremy was out hooking up with every hot babe he could find on campus, I was back in the dorms, staying focused and studying. I was determined to get my business degree and make my parents proud.

Echoes of my devastation hit me as I remember getting the call that they had been in a car crash, killing them both on impact.

I miss them like crazy, but I know they'd be proud of where I am today. I got out with a business degree and a computer science one to boot. So, naturally, I started my own software company and made my first million.

After college, Jeremy returned to the West Coast, where his family lives and where he has a sister he takes care of.

I was pretty lonely in the Big Apple all by myself until Jeremy finally put it to me straight in a way that only a guy's best friend can.

Dude, there's nothing holding you there. Why don't you come out where I'm at?

His words were a huge revelation. It finally dawned on me. Fuck it. I might as well.

At least my best bud will be out here, so I'll have somebody to grab a beer with now and then.

As much as I sound like a loser, I know I could attract willing female companionship if I wanted it. But call me crazy because I'm waiting for that special someone. If I ever settle down with a woman, I want to have what my parents had. I remember the love that surrounded them whenever they were together.

Yeah, that's what I want. A wife, a family, the whole nine yards. All or nothing.

I just don't know if that's in the cards for me. I've never found *the one*.

Maybe she's out here somewhere on the West Coast.

A grin tips the corners of my mouth as I carry the box up to the porch of my new pad.

I almost stumble and fall when a fluffy, cinnamon-colored ball comes zipping around my legs.

"Whoa!" I catch myself just in time.

I steady the box before laying it gently on my porch while regarding the little dog yipping up at me. Her tongue is lolling out of her mouth, which I swear is wide with a grin. She yips at me and stands on her hind legs, waving her front paws at me in supplication.

I chuckle and bend to let her sniff my hand, though it's clear from the way she's dancing up and down that we don't need that formality. This little pup has already decided that she likes me. She doesn't even sniff my hand before giving it a little lick, clearly granting me permission to run my hand over her soft fur. She arches up into my touch more like a cat than a dog, and I chuckle again.

"Trixie!" I hear a soft, feminine voice calling the dog's name in a reprimand.

I look up and go completely still.

Oh my god. The most beautiful creature I've ever seen in my entire life is standing in front of me. She's wearing bright yellow shorts and a navy and white tank top. Her hair is blonde, bleached light by the sun, and flows midway down her back.

She walks closer to me, and my eyes trail up from her flip-flops all the way up those long legs to the most startling pair of blue eyes I've ever seen. They're clearer than a summer day and just as captivating. Pretty pink lips and an upturned nose sit on a round face.

"I'm so sorry!" She apologizes to me for her little pup.

"It's okay. We were just getting acquainted."

The dog pushes her nose into my hand, and I stroke her from the top of her head to the tip of her tail. I pick her up and stand, holding her in my arms.

"I'm Stone," I tell the pretty blonde before me, extending my hand to her. I realize it's a doofus move, shaking her hand, but I'll take any excuse to touch her.

She smiles, the apples of her cheeks dimpling prettily, and I swear I'm a goner.

"I'm Mia," that husky little voice says.

Now that I'm standing at my full height, I tower over her. She's a tiny thing, yet her legs seem to go on forever. How can such a short girl have the longest legs in the world?

She takes my hand with a giggle. The moment our palms touch, liquid fire roars through my veins.

"It looks like you've already met Trixie." She waves toward her dog.

"Yeah, she's cute," I reply, though I'm looking at her and not the dog. "What kind of dog of dog is she?" I know I've seen her type before, but I can't place the breed.

"A Pomeranian," Mia answers before she motions for her dog. "Come here, Trixie."

She holds her arms out, and I transfer the dog to her like I'm transferring a baby to its mother. Our arms brush. It's just the barest brush of her skin against mine, but it's enough to have me hard up in a way I've never been before. Right then, I know. It might seem crazy. It might seem fast. But when you know, you know. It's her. This girl. *Mia*. She's who I've been waiting for. My other half. The one I'm going to spend my life with. The woman I'm going to make mine and have a family with.

Something clicks inside me as I look at her, excitement coursing through my veins.

Mia continues to smile at me, and I grin back at her like an idiot.

I need to invite her in for coffee. Hell, I don't even have my coffee pot set up, but I'll take her out somewhere. We can do anything she wants. I want to be near her and learn more about her. Just as I'm getting ready to invite her in for a coffee, her phone rings.

"Oh, just a sec.." Mia holds up a finger as she pulls her cell phone from her back pocket. "Hello?"

Holding the phone to her ear with one hand, she cradles her fluffy dog in the other arm. She mouths *I'm sorry* at me and then stays silent as she listens to the person on the other end of the line. Huffing out a breath, she rolls her eyes and smiles.

Who is she talking to on the phone? I'm starting to worry that maybe it's a husband or boyfriend.

Mia puts my fears at ease by moving the phone away from her mouth and whispering, "It's my brother.

I'm so sorry, but I have to take this. He's overbearing and overprotective. He thinks he's my dad and not my brother." She releases a frustrated sigh before she continues. "Anyway, welcome to the neighborhood! I'm your next-door neighbor! Well, I'm sure you've figured that out." Her face flushes as she chatters on. "It's nice here. I think you'll like it! We can catch up later."

Before I can tell her how much I'd like that, she's flitting away, her dog under one arm and that phone to her ear. "Yes, I'm listening. I swear!"

I don't know who this overbearing and overprotective brother is, but he's going to have to move over because I've just found my woman, and no brother is going to keep me away from her. He can step down because a new man is in town, and I'll be looking out for Mia.

CHAPTER 2

Mia

I COULD KILL my brother for calling. He *always* calls me at the worst possible time. This time, I was just getting to meet my insanely hot new next-door neighbor. And when I say he's insanely hot, I mean he's melt-your-panties-right-off-you hot. Jason Mamoa hot. Mr. Tall, Dark, and Sexy hot. Mr. Please Take my Virginity hot.

That kinda hot.

Stone.

I'm convinced my brother has a tracker implanted in my ass that alerts him when I'm around a hot guy because he *always* calls and screws it up. Okay, I can't remember the last time I was around a hot guy, but you get my drift.

I can't remember the last time I went out on a date, but that's not the point. It's been forever since I found anyone I wanted to date, but anytime I do, my brother gives them the third degree. You'd think he was my father and not my brother with how overprotective and overbearing he is. I know it's because he loves me. Since we were little kids, our parents were busy traveling the world, so it's always been Jeremy and me for as long as I can remember.

When Mom and Dad weren't around, which was pretty much all the time, Jeremy stepped up and parented me. He's the best big brother ever, and he's certainly gone above and beyond the call of duty as a sibling.

We've always been close. I missed him terribly when he went off to college, but now that he's home, he's about to drive me freaking crazy checking up on me.

He senses danger around every corner.

Talking of danger...

I glance over my shoulder to see Stone still looking at me, his stormy grey eyes intense. The man screams danger and excitement. I don't mean he's dangerous like he'd hurt me—somehow, I just *know* he wouldn't.

No, it's more like the kind of dangerous where fathers wouldn't leave their daughters alone with him. No woman in her right mind could resist a hunk like Stone.

I stroke my hands over Trixie's fur. I could both strangle and kiss her for running outside like that. My rambunctious little puppy has a mind of her own. She loves to run around outside, but I hate it when I open the door and she runs off. I'm scared that she's going to run into the road one day and get hurt.

But this time, it seems she was as enamored with the big sexy man next door as I am.

My god, the man is enormous with bulging muscles that strain against his shirt. His dark hair and brown eyes are as tempting as chocolate, and his square jawline with its bit of stubble is so sexy.

He looked to be at least my brother's age, so that puts him at about seven years older than me.

And my goodness, the way he stroked his hand over Trixie from the top of her head to the tip of her tail. I've never been jealous of my puppy, but I was then.

I give her a halfhearted glare. "You little slut," I tell her with envy, wishing it had been me those gigantic hands had stroked over. Trixie gives me a look that clearly says, *"You're just jealous."*

Damn right I am.

I snort to myself as I imagine my brother trying to give Stone the third degree. My brother may be big and tall, but he's got nothing on Stone. Gosh, even his name sounds hard and masculine. It fits the man because he's built like a fucking stone.

I clench my thighs together involuntarily as I peek out of my window and watch as the man continues to cart box after box into his house.

I consider going out and offering to help him, but he looks like he's got it in hand. Plus, those boxes are nearly as big as I am, so I wouldn't be much help. I'd be in the way, and, let's face it, could I be any more obvious? I don't want to come across as pathetic by throwing myself at some hot guy who probably has beautiful women dripping off both arms.

Still, I can't resist peeking out my window to check if a girlfriend or, God-forbid, a wife joins him.

A shiver of satisfaction goes through me when he finally finishes carrying all his boxes in and I haven't seen a woman come along. I didn't think to check his finger and see if there was a ring there. It doesn't look like he's with anyone, but how is a man like him *not* taken?

I shake my head and step back, running a hand through my hair. What am I doing? I'm just some silly nineteen-year-old girl. Even if he's not in a relation-ship, that's not to say he's going to want anything to do with *me*.

Trixie runs over to the water ball and laps up the water before she flops onto her side and lays there panting like the morning's events were too much for her.

"Yeah, me too, little pup," I sigh, glancing at Stone on his front porch.

He sits in a chair and surveys his lawn while I gape at him and feel like a voyeur eyeing him this way.

I chew on my lip and consider my possibilities. I don't want to look like a fangirl, but I'm tired of never taking chances. Didn't I just tell myself earlier this summer that I'm going to put myself out there more? I started by enrolling in design school—unbeknownst to my brother. Yeah, I can't wait for the conversation we're going to have about that once he finds out I did it without telling him.

But back to my neighbor...I should at least go over and be friendly. We *are* neighbors, so it's not like I'll be flirting with him or anything. I'm just being neighborly.

So, yeah. I'm going over there, and if he's not inter-ested, I'll pick up on it, and that'll be that.

Yeah. I can do this.

I flip my hair over my shoulder and open my front door. I hear Trixie's little paws pitter-pattering over to me, and I turn around and give her a stern, "Stay." She lets out a little whimper, but I shake my head at her. "No, you stay this time. You already had your turn. It's my turn now."

Her little tail drops as she sits on her hind paws, glaring at me. I'm sure she'll puff up and be mad at me for a while, but she'll get over it. She always does. Still, it amazes me how much of an attitude my girl has. She can hold a grudge like a human.

I can't worry about that right now, though.

My house is cute and cozy, a pretty bungalow that's perfect for my puppy and me. Stone's house is a contemporary build, much larger than mine, and all hard, clean lines. It's also a lot more valuable, meaning Stone must be loaded to afford this property.

Not that my brother and I aren't well off. We're not insanely rich, but what our parents sacrificed in time with us, they tried to make up for with the size-able trust funds they set up in our names. We came into them when we turned eighteen, and while I'd rather have had my parents around growing up, I'm more financially stable than most teens my age, thanks to their financial foresight. My parents usually do FaceTime once a year on my birthday to wish me a happy birthday, so it's not like I *never* see them.

I step outside, and Stone's eyes are immediately on me. I feel his gaze across the small expanse separating my house from his, and a tremble teases my spine. He stands and smiles at me as I cross the barrier to him. I give him an awkward wave and apologize again for my brother interrupting our conversation earlier.

"My brother always calls me at the most inconvenient times," I say wryly, shaking my head.

"That's okay." A smile pulls at the corner of his lips.

Good lord, the man's smile is doing odd things to my body. I'm all shaky and buzzy, but in a good way. "I came over to welcome you to the neighborhood officially." I tuck my hair behind my ear nervously and look up at him. Jesus, the man has to be at least six foot four, and I'm all of five foot nothing. He's so big, he could crush me with his bare fist. A little shiver of excitement races through me at that thought.

There's something seriously wrong with me if the idea of being crushed by him is sexy.

"And what a beautiful welcome." My breath catches as his eyes trail from the top of my head to the tip of my toes.

Oh my god.

Is Stone flirting with *me*? I blush with pleasure, suddenly realizing I'm in over my head. Where do I go from here? Am I supposed to flirt back? I don't know how to flirt. What am I supposed to do?

I shift on my feet and smile up at him. "Yeah, so I just wanted to come over and tell you if you ever need some sugar or something, I'm right next door."

His eyes twinkle as he steps off his porch. He closes the remaining space between us until he's standing so close to me that I can feel the heat emanating from his body like the rays of the sun shining down on our heads.

"You offering me some sugar, sweetheart?" The way he calls me *sweetheart* has my legs turning to jelly, and I clasp my hands in front of me to keep them from shaking.

"Well, you know, a *cup* of sugar or whatever people say when someone new moves in next door." I let out a nervous giggle before I hear myself apologizing again. "I'm sorry. I'm horrible at this." I consider bolting, embarrassed beyond measure.

"No, you're not." He reaches out to tuck my hair behind my ear. The brush of his big fingers over my ear has my breath hitching, especially when he trails his knuckles along my cheek.

"If I knew this was the welcome I was going to get,

I'd have moved in sooner," he says, his voice deep and husky.

I blush at his words and the heated look in his eyes. He looks like he's going to say more, but my dreaded phone rings again.

I let out a groan of frustration. "I'm so sorry."

I pull the phone out of the back pocket of my shorts. It's my brother—again.

Stone is still watching me with that heated look. I tell him regretfully, "I'm sorry, but I have to take this because if I don't, he'll send a SWAT team out looking for me."

Stone's eyebrow raises, and his mouth quirks like he thinks I'm joking, but I'm not. My brother is insane about making sure I'm okay.

"Your brother keeps a tight rein on you," he notes with amusement.

"Ha, you have no idea," I sigh.

He chuckles. "Well, I don't blame him. If I had a sister half as pretty as you, I'd be overbearingly over-protective as well."

My face flushes even brighter. I'm sure Stone meant it as a compliment...but did he just equate me to being his sister? I'm confused now and don't know what to think.

"Hello." I'm sure my voice comes out bratty, but damn it, my brother, Jeremy, is getting on my nerves.

Jeremy's voice blares into my ear, "Don't forget, Mia. You're supposed to be here at eight o'clock."

"Of course, I won't forget," I huff.

"I'm serious," he snaps. "No pretending you're sick. This is my best friend from college. He's like a brother to me, so he's your new brother too. I want you to meet him, and I want you to be respectful. I want us all to get along and be one big happy family. The guy doesn't have any family of his own, so we're his family now."

"Okay, Dad," I smart off to him. Geez, Jeremy can be so bossy.

"Very funny." I hear the smile in his voice as he picks up on my irritation. For some reason, Jeremy thinks it's funny when I joke that he's like my father. I think he takes it as a sign that he's doing his job right.

"Make sure you're not late," he adds.

I don't even dignify that statement with a response before hanging up the phone.

Stone is regarding me curiously.

"Sorry. I have to go. I have to do something with my brother."

"Don't worry about it," Stone reassures me. "I have someplace to be tonight too."

I can't help but wonder if he's got a date. Oh, my

God, if he does, I've just made myself look like a complete fool coming over here and attempting to flirt with him.

I don't know if he can read the emotions flitting across my face, but his next words put me at ease. "I'm meeting up with an old buddy."

I relax. An old buddy. Not a female because most people wouldn't call their female friends buddies, would they? Isn't that like a guy thing?

Anyway, I don't have time to sit here and ponder. I toss a shy goodbye at him before I awkwardly turn and make my way across the yard to my house.

"Until later, Mia," Stone's deep voice rumbles from behind me. "I'll be seeing you around."

I smile to myself as I close my door. Yes, I guess he will, considering he lives right next door.

It's funny. Earlier I was telling myself I was going to get out more, but now I'm thinking that hanging around the house for the next few weeks sounds like a perfect idea.

CHAPTER 3

Stone

I'M HUMMING as I pull up to Jeremy's place. I get out of the car and practically skip up his steps, feeling lighter than I have in years. California is turning out to be great so far.

I ring the doorbell, and a second later, my buddy opens the door, grinning from ear to ear.

"Stone! Good to see you, man. It's been too long."

We've kept in touch via text and phone calls, but it's been a good minute since we've seen each other in the flesh. Jeremy has filled out some, as I know I have. All that time alone gave me the opportunity to work out and buff up for lack of anything else to do.

"Man, all that working out is going to help you land the babes," Jeremy says with a wink as he appraises me frankly. "You're built like a brick shithouse."

I give him an affectionate push. "Speak for yourself, man. You're not quite as scrawny as I remember."

Jeremy thrusts his chest out and practically struts like a peacock. "I hit the gym every day. Like I said, the babes out here love a muscled chest." He wiggles his eyebrows at me suggestively, and I chuckle. Same old Jeremy.

"What do you say we hit the club together later?" Jeremy asks.

I shake my head, opening my mouth to tell him that there'll be no clubbing in my imminent future because I met the girl of my dreams earlier. My mouth snaps closed when I hear a suspiciously familiar voice floating down the hallway toward us.

"Jeremy? Is he here yet?"

Her voice sounds adorably whiny, and my breath catches as she saunters into the room and then stops dead in her tracks, her eyes widening.

"Mia," Jeremy begins, "I want you to meet my buddy—"

"Stone," she finishes.

His eyebrows furrow as he looks between us in

confusion. "Wait. You two know each other? *How* do you two know each other?"

I hurry to answer his question before he gets the wrong idea and goes apeshit. Holy hell, *Jeremy* is the overbearing, overprotective brother. It makes total sense because if there's one thing I know about Jeremy, it's how protective he is of his little sister. He talked about her all the time when we were roommates in college. In all those years, I never saw a picture of her or knew anything about her beyond her name. How the hell I've never put it together before this is beyond me.

Mia has the same name as Jeremy's sister Mia. Why didn't I see it before? My best friend's *little sister* is my next-door neighbor. *Fuck!*

"I met her this morning when I was moving in. Her puppy assaulted me." I crack a half-smile at her to try to break the ice.

Jeremy grumbles, "That dog is a menace. I tried to get her to let me put the little mutt in obedience school, but she won't do it."

"Hey!" She frowns at him. "Trixie is a free spirit."

I fight back a grin at her response.

"Disobedient, more like it," Jeremy mumbles with a frown.

Mia sticks her tongue out at him like a child,

making me chuckle. God, she's adorable. It only makes her more endearing to see her act like a brat to her brother. They're true siblings—something I never had.

Jeremy cuts a look at me. "You know, this is perfect, bro. Since you're living right next door to my sister, you can keep an eye on her for me. Let me know if any dudes come over."

Mia cuts daggers at her brother, "You do realize I'm nineteen, Jeremy, and you're not my father? I can date whoever I want, whenever I want."

Jeremy gives her a hard look. "Not until they go through me first." His eyes soften. "I want to make sure nobody takes advantage of you, Mia."

I interrupt them. "She's safe with me." Jeremy doesn't even have to ask. There's no way in hell I'm letting another man into Mia's house.

Jeremy looks at me approvingly and claps me on the shoulder.

My conscience pricks at me. Jeremy would be upset if he knew why his best friend was so willing to watch out for his sister.

Mia's eyes cut to me. She blushes even as she lifts her chin defiantly. "I don't need anyone to look out for me. I can take care of myself."

I remember how adorable she was when she came

over to offer me some sugar earlier. If she only knew the kind of sugar I want from her...

I glance at Jeremy. He's the best friend I've ever had. He's like family, so Mia is supposed to be like my sister. I know Jeremy would *not* be okay with me wanting to bang his little sister. I think that violates all sorts of bro codes.

"You see anything suspicious, you let me know," Jeremy tells me as if Mia didn't speak.

Mia all but stomps her foot in anger as she hisses at him, "I told you I don't need a bodyguard. I have Trixie."

Jeremy scoffs, "When I told you to get a guard dog, I didn't mean something the size of a peanut."

Mia crosses her arms and rushes to defend her spirited little Pom. "Trixie may be small, but she's ferocious, and she would protect me if someone were trying to hurt me."

She must have heard her name because Trixie comes trotting into the room. She growls at Jeremy, clearly taking her mistress's side in the matter. She spots me and comes running over, wagging her tail happily like she did earlier. I don't know why this little puppy loves me so much. I bend down to scratch behind her ears, and she promptly flops onto her back, exposing her belly. I chuckle and oblige her with a belly rub.

"Oh, man, you're a sucker for her too," Jeremy groans.

"You're just jealous that Trixie sees through your bullshit and doesn't like you," Mia tells him smugly.

"Whatever." Jeremy shakes his head. "Are we gonna sit here and make out over your little pipsqueak dog all night, or are we going to eat so that Stone and I can hit up the club?"

Mia's eyes widen as she glances at me and quickly looks away.

Shit.

I have no interest in going to a club and open my mouth to say as much when Mia speaks.

"Seeing as how your old college buddy and I have met, I don't see why it's important we have dinner together to get to know one another. We're next-door neighbors, so I'm sure we'll be seeing plenty of each other. You guys go on to the club. I'll be fine."

She picks up Trixie, and her flip-flops slap against the tile as she heads toward the door.

Jeremy raises an eyebrow at me, pleased with Mia's response. "Works for me. We can get something at the bar, man." He shouts after Mia. "Make sure you eat something tonight, Mia! Something nutritious—not just mac and cheese or pizza."

"Sure thing, Dad!" she calls back sarcastically.

The front door slams behind her, resonating through my entire body with a finality that fills me with dread. It's just my luck that the only girl I've ever wanted happens to be my best bro's little sister.

Fuck me.

What am I going to do?

CHAPTER 4

Mia

I AM SUCH AN IDIOT. Not only is Stone my brother's best friend from college, but they're going clubbing tonight.

Stone *was* laughing at me earlier. I was wrong when I thought he was flirting with me. He was humoring me, making fun of me.

He's into women more his age with more experience. I may be naïve, but I'm not as naïve as my brother thinks. I know Jeremy gets around and plays the field, so it's ironic as hell that he believes he has the right to tell me what I can and can't do.

It's none of his business, but I'm sure he'd be

pleased to know that his baby sis is still a virgin. I'm not saving myself for marriage or anything. I've just never found anyone I wanted to give myself to that way. But my little lady bits came alive for Stone, and I thought he might be the one who finally made me a woman.

That all just flew out the window. I was stupid about the whole thing.

"God, did I really walk next door and offer him a cup of sugar?" I ask my little pup.

Trixie looks at me with her tongue hanging out of her mouth.

"Why am I asking you? You're a bigger slut for Stone than I am." The only difference is Trixie can get away with it because she's a cute puppy.

I'm just going to have to forget about Stone. That's all there is to it. He's my brother's best friend, and he's not interested in a girl like me. Technically, I'm still a teenager.

I groan when I think of Stone telling my brother about my ridiculous ass coming over and offering to lend him a cup of sugar.

My brother will probably lose his shit if he finds out I have a crush on his best friend.

Wait, I do *not* have a crush on him. I just met the guy, and yeah, he's insanely hot, but so what? That's all there is to it.

I'm just going to stay in my yard, and he can stay in his. This won't be a problem. I can be a mature adult about this.

I take a deep breath and tell Trixie, "I'm nineteen and fixing to go to fashion school. I have to stay focused on my career."

When I get home, Trixie hits the food and water bowl while I pull out my charcoals and my sketch pad and get back to what I love doing best—sketching out some new designs.

I do not think about the new guy who just moved in next door. I definitely don't look out the window when I hear his car pull in around midnight because I don't care when he comes home.

It's none of my business how late he stays out.

Still, I notice that he comes home alone.

———

"Trixie!" I call my fluffy ball of terror as she makes her escape.

I tried to slip out of the door to water my daisies, but Trixie was as fast as lightning when she heard the doorknob turn.

"Come back here!"

She ignores me, running from my yard to next door where Stone is lifting...well...stones.

He's laying them in a ring to create what looks like a flower bed. My mouth goes dry when he stands to his full height. He's not wearing a shirt, and his muscles ripple with every move. It's hot as hell today, and beads of sweat glisten on his skin as they roll over the ridges of his chest and abdomen.

Okay, so I've never been one of those girls who get off on hot, sweaty guys. Sweat, in general, is kind of disgusting, but this is Stone, so can I help it that I want to lick those beads of sweat from his firm skin?

Yeah, that's gross. But tell that to my hormones because my vagina has perked up the way Trixie does when she hears the crinkle of a food wrapper.

"Hey, girl," Stone greets my pup as she runs over and jumps on his leg, begging for his attention.

He bends over to give her a few strokes on the head before he stands and wipes his brow with the back of his arm.

Sweet baby Jesus. The man is a god. He looks like one of those statues famous sculptors create. The man is a work of art.

I put my hands on my hips, reprimanding my wild dog. I'm pissed off at her for getting me out here to lust after Stone—the one man I can't have. If my brother has his way, I'll end up with a man handpicked by him.

"Oh, she's okay," Stone chuckles as he looks over at me

"No, she's not. I swear she's a whore for you."

If possible, his grin only widens. "A whore for me, you say?"

My face turns a furious shade of red. Okay, that was a horrible word choice. Now it sounds like I'm thinking of him and sex in the same thought, which I *am*, but I don't need to let him know that.

Stone looks down at Trixie affectionately before he bends and picks her up in his big arms. She nuzzles her head into his chest, and I'm envious of my dog when Stone strokes his hand from the top of her head to the tip of her tail in the way she loves. She might as well be a cat because I can practically hear her purring and shamelessly drooling all over him.

"She just knows I'll stroke her right," Stone tells me with a huge grin. He looks directly into my eyes, his dark gaze heated with innuendo.

Heat infuses my body. Oh, my god, is he flirting with me? Does he want me after all? Even knowing that I'm his best friend's little sister?

But then I remember how he went clubbing with

my brother last night. "Oh, I'm sure you know how to stroke all the girls."

Stone's eyebrows shoot into his hairline as I walk over to him and primly take my pup from him. I'm being rude, but I don't know how to take him when he's flirting with me one minute, and the next, he's out with my brother picking up babes. It shouldn't piss me off, but it does.

"Did you have fun at the club last night?" I ask casually, petting Trixie as she kicks in my arms, trying to get back to Stone. The little traitor.

He looks at me for a long moment before he answers. "No, I left way before your brother."

I blink in shock. "I thought you guys were best friends?"

Stone chuckles. "We are, but that doesn't mean we're glued at the hip or that I'm going to hang around while he picks out random babes when I'm not interested."

"Not interested," I repeat like a parrot.

"Yeah, that's right."

"Oh?" I say, feigning nonchalance as I absently stroke Trixie. She keeps casting longing glances at Stone. I'm starting to believe my dog would leave me for him. I'd be hurt if I didn't understand her sentiment.

My eyes widen as I as a thought occurs to me. "Wait, are you gay?"

Stone scowls. "What? Jesus, no." He shakes his head and closes the distance between us. He's so close I can smell his cologne and his natural masculine scent. It's a heady concoction that makes me dizzy.

I look up at him, and his eyes lock on mine. "I have everything I need right here at home."

My breath hitches. Is he implying what I think he's implying? He could just be saying that he doesn't want the complication of a woman and he can take care of his needs by himself.

God, I'm overthinking everything.

My eyes widen when his face moves closer to mine. Is he going to kiss me?

I never find out because his phone rings, pulling us from our trance.

I take a step back as he glances at his phone and frowns. "It's your brother."

"You should take it." I give him my brightest smile. "And I'm sorry about Trixie. I'll try to keep a better leash on her."

Before Stone can say anything, I turn and march back to my yard. I remind myself that Stone is off-limits, which sucks because not only is he ridiculously hot, but my puppy is in love with him. She whimpers, looking back at him like I'm breaking her heart.

"Oh, get over it," I snap at her. I immediately regret my harsh tone when she turns those big puppy dog eyes on me. "I'm sorry, girl." I pet her behind her ears and place a kiss on her head. "I know you can't help how you feel," I tell her, glancing across the yard to where Stone is standing shirtless, talking on the phone to my brother.

I can't either.

CHAPTER 5

Stone

I SPEND the next few days trying not to think about my best friend's little sister, which is hard when she lives right next door, and I'm constantly glancing over there, hoping for a glimpse of her. It doesn't help that she wears skimpy little shorts and tank tops, showing off that perfect body.

I love it when she wears her hair flowing to her waist, but I also love it when she gathers it up in a long ponytail. Something about that ponytail...I imagine fisting it in my hand with my cock down her throat and those pretty blue eyes looking up at me. I groan as I jerk myself to release at the tantalizing vision.

Jeremy would kill me if he knew how I was stroking myself off every day to thoughts of his sister, but hell, it's either this or go over there and bury myself inside her.

It's fucked up. I come harder than I ever have thinking about Mia and then immediately feel guilty—especially when I remember the deep conversation Jeremy had with me about his sister.

He told me he worries about her because she's too trusting. When Mia turned eighteen, he took her to Vegas even though she couldn't legally drink or gamble. They were walking along the street and some dude started talking to her, offering her a job. Mia being the sweet person she is, didn't realize he was a pimp trying to pick her up.

I don't even have to tell you how the rest of that story went. It ended with Jeremy's fist in the man's face.

"And that's just the thing about Mia," Jeremy told me. "She's too trusting. She's so innocent and very impressionable. I practically raised her. I know she's my little sister, man, but she might as well be my daughter the way I worry about her."

Maybe that's fucked up, but it's a sweet kind of fucked up. Jeremy is a fantastic brother, and I'm proud as hell of him for stepping up to raise his sister when his parents were busy touring the world.

But it also means that if I tell Jeremy my true interest in Mia, it would be like saying I want to fuck his daughter. How messed up is that?

But I don't just want to fuck her.

It's so much more than that. I want to take care of her. I want to marry her. I want everything with her. I may not have known her long, but I feel this soul-deep connection with her.

Jeremy also told me how flighty she is. He claims she gets in and out of things and never sticks with anything. When she was growing up, she wanted to do cheerleading one week, and the next, she wanted to play basketball. She could never stick with one thing.

"Maybe she was just trying to find herself," I told him.

He shook his head. "The most consistent she's ever been is with that dog. That's the one thing she's stuck with."

I didn't say anything else. I just listened to Jeremy as he rambled on about his worries. If only he knew how I would take care of her and that he'd never have to worry about her again. I considered approaching him and asking him for his blessing to date his sister.

But what if he said no? Hell, he'd shoot me if he knew the thoughts I was having about her.

So, I do my best and tell myself that she's off-limits. I try to tell myself that she's too young for me, but I know that's not true. I couldn't give a fuck how old she is.

I need to keep my paws off her, but it's hard when her pup runs into my yard every time she escapes. I tell myself I'm going to be cool whenever we're thrown together, but I always end up flirting with her. It's like I have no filter when I'm around her. I can't hide my true feelings for her. I've come *so* close to kissing her more times than I can count.

And I notice the flushed look on her face whenever we talk. I'm sure she wants me too, but she's holding back for the same reason I am.

There's a big elephant between us, and his name is Jeremy.

I stand up from my porch chair when I see Mia emerge from her house, holding Trixie in her arms.

That's not why I stand up, though, nor is it why my eyes about bug out of my head.

She's wearing nothing but an itty bitty, teeny weeny, yellow polka dot bikini. I've never seen someone wear a bikini from the song, but Mia is rocking it.

The girl is always wearing yellow. It must be her favorite color, and it suits her because it's such a bright, happy, bubbly color—just like her.

That bikini is so small that her tits are about to fall out, and the spectacular globes of her ass are on full display, cupped like ripe peaches.

I haven't once made good on my promise to Jeremy to call him if I see anything suspicious, nor have I butted into Mia's life in any way, but I'm sure as hell going to now. There is no way she's leaving the house dressed like that.

"Mia!" I call over to her.

She looks over at me with black sunglasses shielding her eyes. "Hey!" She gives me a big wave and a bright smile.

I crook my finger at her in a come-hither motion.

She comes prancing right over, her tits jiggling in those tiny triangles of fabric. My dick hardens as I try not to ogle her.

Trixie is straining in her arms to get to me. Mia puts the Pomeranian down with a huff, and the dog runs over to me. I bend over and give her a cursory pat on the head before fixing my full attention back on Mia.

"Where are you going?" I ask her.

Her brow furrows. "I'm wearing a bikini, silly, so

I'm going to the beach." She shakes her head and laughs. "Seriously. What's up with you, Stone?"

I look down at her, my throat working as I take in her almost-naked body. "You cannot go to the beach dressed like that," I croak.

She frowns and crosses her arms. The action pushes the globes of her breasts together to create more cleavage.

I'm standing here fighting the biggest boner of my life as I try not to jizz in my pants while staring at my best friend's little sister.

"Newsflash, Stone. Bikinis are what women wear to the beach," she tells me playfully.

"I don't care what you call it," I say frankly. "That's just a scrap of fabric that doesn't cover anything, and I don't think your brother would be okay with this."

Mia scoffs and uncrosses her arms before she raises her chin defiantly. "Is that what this is about? Look, Stone, I think you're taking this bodyguard thing too seriously. You don't have to report everything you see around here to my brother. I promise I won't tell if you don't." She smiles at me sweetly and bats her eyelashes.

I promise I won't tell if you don't.

That conjures up images of our naked bodies

doing things I should not be thinking about doing with my best friend's little sister.

"It's not just your brother," I finally growl. "I don't think it's appropriate either."

Her eyes widen as she blinks at me self-consciously. "You don't like it?" she asks as she looks down at herself in complete confusion.

Jeremy is right. She's so innocent she doesn't see what's wrong with this picture.

"Mia," I speak to her very slowly. "You have no idea what seeing you in such a skimpy little bikini like that does to men."

She blinks up at me again. "What does it do?" she asks, her voice barely more than a whisper.

I swallow hard. "It makes them think about things."

She cocks her head to the side. "What kinds of things?"

Fuck, she's killing me. I fight back a groan as my cock presses up against my zipper. "If you have to ask, you shouldn't be wearing that bikini."

Her mouth opens as if she's going to say something else, but the sound of a car distracts her, and I turn to see Jeremy pulling into my driveway.

Jeremy has one foot out of the car when he spots

Mia. His eyes darken and he shakes his head. "No way," he tells her as he points back at her house. "You're not going out like that."

"I just got done telling her that," I tell him dryly.

He nods at me in approval. "See? We're in agreement on this. Thanks, buddy." He turns his stern gaze back to his sister.

Mia crosses her arms and huffs. "Neither one of you is in any position to tell me what to do."

"I'm not in the mood to argue with you, Mia," Jeremy warns her.

She glares at him.

The mailman chooses that moment to come walking up the sidewalk. He spots Mia and can barely pull his eyes away from her as he gives her the mail.

Jeremy and I both glare at him while he gapes at her.

"Hey!" Jeremy snaps at him. "That's my little sister."

The mailman's eyes widen before he quickly averts them and hurries on down the street.

Jeremy raises an eyebrow at Mia. "See?"

"See what?" she asks in exasperation.

"The mailman. Or did you not notice how he was ogling you?"

Mia just blinks at him innocently.

I let out an incredulous laugh. She doesn't recognize the effect she has on men. She looks between Jeremy and me as we share a knowing glance.

"That right there is why you can't go out alone looking like that," Jeremy tells her stubbornly. "You don't even see it."

"See what?" she asks again in frustration, shaking her head. "Never mind. You guys are freaking ridiculous. Trixie loves going to the beach, and this is what I'm wearing. Trixie!" For once, Trixie listens to her and leaves me to go bounding over, no doubt lured in by the promise of the beach.

Mia bends over to pick up her pup and drops some of her mail on the ground. Jeremy grabs it for her, and his jaw tightens as his eyes settle on one of the letters.

Mia's body tenses.

"The Institute for Design and Fashion? What's this, Mia?"

Mia sighs. "I was going to tell you."

"When?" Jeremy runs a weary hand over his eyes and doesn't give her a chance to answer. "Mia, this isn't like one of your extracurricular activities in high school. Choosing a career is a big deal. It's not something that you can just throw yourself into."

"I know that," she hisses at him. "I've thought long and hard about this. I love fashion, and I'm good at coming up with designs. Everyone says so." Her eyes take on a vulnerable look. "Jeremy, I really want to do this."

Jeremy cuts her off with a harsh laugh. "Yeah, you want to do this now, Mia, but what about next week? It'll be something else like it always is. You flit from one thing to another and never stick with anything. I don't want to see you wasting money and time signing up for something that you're not even going to want to do next week."

Mia's face falls and tears shimmer in her eyes. Jeremy's words came off pretty harsh.

"I am not a child anymore, Jeremy. You are not my father, and you cannot tell me what to do." Mia's tone is icy even as her voice wobbles. "You know what sucks? I didn't come to you because I knew this is what you would say. I knew you wouldn't believe in me. You always treat me like I'm still a stupid little girl. Well, guess what? I'm not. I'm an adult, and you need to start treating me like one." She shakes her head as the tears spill over and run down her cheeks. "It hurts that my own brother doesn't believe in me and thinks I'm a total flake."

"Mia," Jeremy begins wearily, "that's not what I said."

"You didn't have to say it." Her pain is palpable as she turns and walks into the house, slamming the door behind her

I guess the beach trip is off.

"Fuck!" Jeremy shouts in frustration, scrubbing a hand over his face. He looks at me as if suddenly remembering I'm here. "I should go talk to her."

I hold out a hand to stop him. "No offense, bro, but I think you're the last person she wants to talk to right now."

Jeremy's shoulders slump. "You think I should give her some time?"

"Definitely."

He exhales a breath before running a hand through his hair. "I guess I'll go home then. Listen, will you keep an eye on her for me?"

I nod at him. "Always."

His shoulders relax the tiniest bit. "Thanks, Stone. I feel better knowing that you're around for her."

I wait for Jeremy to get in his car and leave, and then I march across the yard and up Mia's porch before knocking on her door. There's no way I can leave her alone when she's upset like this. I have to check on her and make sure she's okay. The thought of her upset and crying is like a cloud dimming the sun. Mia should be bright and happy—not downcast.

I'm here to check on her and help her patch things up with her brother.

Nothing more.

CHAPTER 6

Stone

WHEN MIA OPENS THE DOOR, she looks up at me with tears shimmering in her eyes. God, she looks so beautiful, even when she's crying. It's all I can do not to pull her into my arms and kiss her tears away.

"Mind if I come in?" I ask gruffly.

She doesn't answer verbally but steps back to allow me to pass over the threshold into her home. I glance around the space. It's cute and colorful and fashionable —just like the angel standing in front of me.

"Your brother worries about you, Mia," I begin.

She cuts me off by holding up a hand. "If you came

here to smooth things over between Jeremy and me, just don't."

I close my mouth and nod. "That's not the only reason I came over." I take a step toward her. "I came over to check on you." My eyes scan her beautiful, sad face, and my heart squeezes in my chest. "Are you okay?"

She lets out a humorless laugh. "Of course, I am. Why wouldn't I be okay? My brother doesn't believe in me. Big deal. He never has. He thinks I'm stupid, silly, flighty little Mia."

"But you're not," I finish for her. "You're all grown up, and Jeremy needs to stop babying you."

She nods her head, and I fight back a groan. My eyes rake over her the gentle curves of her body. Fuck yes, she's grown up.

She looks up at me suspiciously. "What? You're not taking his side?"

I exhale a breath. "I was never taking sides to begin with, Mia."

"But my bikini—"

I silence her by pressing a finger against her puffy lips, feeling the sensation all the way down to my cock, which swells even harder in my pants. "I had a problem with the bikini before your brother showed up. Remember?"

arms. "I've wanted to do that since the day I first saw you," I confess as I skate my lips along her jaw and up to her ear, placing gentle kisses against the lobe.

She tilts her head to the side and whimpers. "So why didn't you?"

That question is a reality check slapping me right in the face. I look down at her, groaning as I fight to hold myself back. "You know why," I growl.

"My brother," she states flatly.

I don't answer, dropping my forehead to hers.

"We don't have to tell him right away," she suggests desperately.

I pull back to look at her incredulously. Her cheeks are pink, and her lips are puffy and swollen from my kisses. The knowledge that she wants this just as badly as I do is enough to make me willing to risk my friendship with her brother.

"I don't want you to be a dirty little secret, Mia," I tell her. "If we do this, we'll have to tell him eventually."

Mia peers up at me shyly. "It'll be our secret. Just for a little while. Until Jeremy realizes I'm an adult. Jesus, you saw how he reacted to me choosing a career without talking to him first."

I think of how much he'll flip his shit if he finds out I banged his little sister.

"Please, Stone," she begs me. "I don't want to be a virgin forever while I wait for my overbearing brother to back off."

"Christ," I swear as I close my eyes at the confirmation of what I already suspected. "You're a virgin."

Mia's cheeks flush. "I'm sorry. I've never—"

I grab both of her hands in mine and pull them up to place kisses on her knuckles. "Don't ever apologize for saving yourself for me. I'm thrilled you've never been with anyone else. Do you hear me?"

She nods at me wordlessly before she whispers, "I knew the first day I saw you that you were the one I wanted to give my virginity to."

"You're killing me, Mia," I groan at her admission.

I grab her hips and grind my swollen length into her like a crazed beast. The sweetest virgin in the world is telling me that she's been over here pining for me to pop that little cherry.

"You've been saving that little cherry for me, haven't you, sweetheart?" I don't give her a chance to answer before I take her lips in another deep kiss, all thoughts of her brother swept from my mind. Fuck Jeremy. He'll have to deal with it. There's no way I can turn this girl down, and I would challenge him to do differently if he met the woman he knew was his life.

I trail kisses down the column of Mia's throat,

sucking and licking her neck, though I'm careful not to leave any marks behind. I burn to mark her, but her brother doesn't need to see a hickey on her neck.

I find the bow behind her neck and give it a yank to undo her bikini top. The triangle scraps slide down to reveal her perfectly ripe nipples.

"Look at these pretty little titties," I say reverently, falling to my knees and worshiping them in earnest, sucking and licking at them, savoring every gasp and moan from Mia's throat.

I'm hard as steel in my pants and leaking a steady stream of precum, but I ignore my swollen discomfort, more intent on giving my precious angel pleasure. This girl is a gift, and I intend to treasure her.

"Do you like that, honey?"

Mia moans in answer.

"Has anybody else ever tasted these little cherries?" I know the answer but want to hear it from her lips.

"No," she tells me with a little shake of her head, her eyes still closed as she gives herself over to the sensation.

I grab onto her hips as I growl against her skin, "Good girl."

She moans even louder at the praise, and I file that tidbit away for future reference. She likes being my "good girl." If it causes the sweet noises she's making now, I'll say it every day for the rest of our lives.

I squeeze her ass, kissing every inch of her stomach. Finally, I can't take it anymore and undo the ties on either side of her hips that hold up her sorry excuse for bikini bottoms. The flimsy fabric that wouldn't even cover my balls flutters to the ground, revealing her mouthwatering mound.

I inhale deeply before I run a finger along her slit. She's soaking wet and her juices coat my hand. *Christ Almighty.* "Look how wet you are for me, baby. This pussy is mine, isn't it?"

"Stone!"

The way my name drips from her lips sends desire pulsing hotly through my veins, and a stream of release shoots from my swollen head to stain the inside of my boxers.

I take my first lick, and her flavor explodes on my tongue. She tastes like *mine.* Every inch of her. Everything about her. *Mine.*

She's honey-sweet, and I lick her up, paying attention to every twitch and moan of her body as she fists her fingers in my hair. I grip her thighs tightly and keep going, licking and sucking at her as she pants my name.

"Stone! Something is...I don't know..." She blabbers

incoherently.

She's close. I push a finger gently inside her, increasing the suction on her bundle of nerves. I groan as she flies over the edge, screaming my name and convulsing around my finger. I lick up every drop of her honied release, my chest swelling with pride that I've given her an orgasm—the first orgasm she's ever experienced. Mine is the only tongue to taste her sweetness. And you can bet your ass my mouth is the only one that will ever pleasure her like this.

"Fuck, Mia." I hoist her up into my arms. "I've got to have you now, baby."

She bobs her head up and down, giving me permission. I free myself from my pants, my cock bobbing between us and pressing against her dripping wet hole like a homing missile that knows its target.

I carry her over to her couch and sit down with her straddling me. She hovers above my aching length. I take her face in my hands and kiss her deeply, my chest thrumming in anticipation.

"I'll go slow, baby. Anything you need, you tell me. I'm going to take care of you. You hear me?"

"Stone," Mia says my name softly as she searches my eyes before kissing me sweetly.

Her lips are like a delicate butterfly landing on me, and I sit perfectly still as I accept her favor. She wiggles on me, and I feel her juices flowing down my length. I lower her a little until the head pops in.

Mia's eyes go wide as she looks at me. "Oh, my god, you feel huge."

I chuckle. "What every man wants to hear, baby." I know she isn't saying it to stroke my ego. She's being her authentic self as always.

"It's going to hurt a little bit," I warn her. "But I promise I'll make it all better, honey. Do you trust me?"

She bites her lip and nods. "Yes, I trust you, Stone."

If I didn't already know I was in love with her, I do now. Mia giving me her trust feels better than winning the lottery. It's everything.

The weight of responsibility settles on my shoulders, and I'm determined to make this experience good for her. My pleasure will always take a backseat to hers.

My breathing becomes ragged and sweat breaks out on my brow. Just having her muscles squeeze the tip of me is enough to make me spill. It's taking everything in me to hold back, but I can do this for her.

"Do you want to go slow, or do you just want to get it over with?" I ask through gritted teeth.

She looks down between us where we're

connected, and moisture rushes up my shaft at the wonder on her face. It's sexy as fuck.

"Is it hard for you to sit still? I read somewhere that it's hard for a man to, you know, not move," she tells me innocently.

My heart swells. Fuck, this beautiful, precious girl. She's the one who has to experience the pain of being stretched open for the first time, yet she's worried about me.

I shake my head and try to focus. "This isn't about me, Mia. It's about you. I'll do whatever you want."

She looks down at us for a moment longer before she lifts her eyes to mine. "Just do it."

"Are you sure? Because once I start, there's not going to be any stopping, honey. Once I slip inside that sweet heaven between your thighs, I'll be gone."

She doesn't hesitate before her head bobs up and down, her hair rippling with the movement. I can't wait to see it falling all around her as I bounce her up and down on this dick. "I'm sure, Stone. Make me yours."

Make me yours is what does it. I grab onto her hips and push up into her with a loud shout. I feel her resistance breaking as I slide into her incredibly hot, tight heat. My eyes roll back in my head, and I fight for control.

Mia sucks in a breath and buries her head against my neck.

I place my hand on the back of her head, stroking my fingers through her hair soothingly as her body adjusts to me. "Good girl. You did so good. Fuck, you feel incredible, Mia. So perfect. You were made for me. Feel how you fit around me like a glove? Taking everything in me not to bust up in you right now."

She doesn't answer me. She sits there, clinging to me as I continue speaking endearments to her and praising her. I can't help it. My words are being ripped directly from my soul. I couldn't stop them if I tried. My true feelings are exposed to her, everything I've been fighting from the moment I saw her.

Mia is the one to make the first move. She lifts up and slides back down on me gently. "Oh, that feels good," she moans before doing it again.

"Fuck, yes, it does, baby," I agree, holding her hips and moving into her harder and faster until she's bouncing up and down on me.

"Look at you, good girl, bouncing up and down on your man's dick." I look between us and watch her pussy as it sucks my cock in over and over again. I swear I've never seen a more beautiful sight. "You like that, baby? You like feeling my big dick splitting your little virgin pussy in half?"

She clenches around me at my words. Fuck, my perfect girl loves it when I talk dirty to her.

"Oh god, Stone!" Mia cries out as her release floods me.

"Mia," I growl out as I continue to slam up into her.

"Stone!" she screams my name as she comes on me for the first time.

Her release triggers my own. I hammer my hips up into her as the first gush of my seed tears up my stalk. "Fuck, Mia!"

Somewhere in the back of my mind, it registers that we didn't use a condom. I could get her pregnant and *fuck me* if that thought doesn't send more cum spurting out of my dick.

Mia collapses against me, clinging to me as she buries her face in my neck. Having her in my arms like this feels so right.

I hold her close, still buried inside her as we come down from our release.

Fuck, I'm never going to let her go now.

Never.

She's mine.

CHAPTER 7

Mia

"DO YOU LIKE THEM?" I ask Stone, studying his expression carefully. I don't want him to tell me what he thinks I want to hear because we just had sex. I want to know his honest opinion.

Stone looks up from my sketchbook, his gaze fixed on mine. "I'm no fashion expert, Mia, but even I can see that these are good."

Stone isn't lying to me. I can see it there in his eyes, and I can't stop the smile that breaks across my face as I clap my hands together under my chin. "You mean it?" I already know he does, but it'll make me feel better to hear the confirmation.

"Yeah, Mia. Have you ever showed your brother this?" He looks up at me with a raised eyebrow.

I shake my head and look down. "No. Even if Jeremy thinks they're good, he is right about my history of flitting from one thing to another. I guess I can't blame him for not taking me seriously."

"You were a kid, for Christ's sake, Mia. He can't hold that against you forever." Stone takes my hands in both of his. " I believe in you, baby. You just need to believe in yourself."

My heart warms when he says he believes in me. It's a good feeling. I stand on my tiptoes, pulling his head down to kiss him gently.

"Mmm," he hums against my lips as he kisses me back. "What was that for?"

"For believing in me," I tell him honestly. "For coming over and popping my cherry."

A huge grin breaks across his face. "If your brother only knew how long I wanted to pop it, he'd have shot me by now."

"Our relationship is none of Jeremy's business, nor is my virginity," I point out.

Stone nods. "I get that, but he's my best friend, Mia, and he's entitled to some answers." He lifts my hands to his lips and kisses my knuckles. I love it when he does that. "What I feel for you isn't going away, Mia.

I don't want you thinking this was some one-night stand. I'm in this for the long haul. You know that, right?"

My cheeks flush with pleasure and I smile, my heart soaring. I honestly didn't know if Stone would want me to be his girlfriend, but even if all he wanted was one night—or afternoon—with me, I don't regret him taking my virginity.

"I'm keeping you," he tells me as he nuzzles into my neck.

"When are you going to tell my brother?"

He frowns. "Soon because I can't keep you a secret for very long. We can't be in the same room together without him noticing how I look at you."

"And how's that?" I ask him with a teasing smile.

He lets out a little growl as he pulls me close. "Like you're mine." He kisses the side of my neck." Like I want to mark every inch of your skin with hickeys."

I know that hickeys aren't pretty, but why does the thought of him marking me that way send a rush of pleasure crashing through me?

Trixie gives a little bark of indignation and pushes her furry body between us. I don't know where she was when we were making love, but she made herself scarce. Maybe dogs have some instinct about those things, although she's certainly making her presence known now.

"I think she still wants to go to the beach," I tell him with a raised eyebrow.

His eyes darken as he glances over at my discarded bikini on the floor. "Do you have to wear that?" He glares at the garment like he wants to set it on fire.

I glance over at the tiny pieces of fabric, still not seeing what the big deal is. "No," I concede. "I have a one-piece I can put on."

Stone nods approvingly. "Let's see that one, and how about I take you?"

I smile up at him. "I don't know," I hedge playfully. "Is it okay if he comes, girl?" I ask Trixie.

She gives a little yip and nuzzles Stone's leg, letting me know that she's more than okay with it.

"I guess," I tell Stone. "Trix says you can come."

"Hey, I've had her approval since day one," Stone says smugly.

I giggle. That's true, and it tells me everything I need to know because don't dogs have some sort of internal instinct about people? They say if your dog doesn't like someone, you should stay away from them. But Trixie loved Stone the moment she saw him, which tells me he must be a good one.

I have to talk to my brother at some point, but for now, I'm just going to enjoy my time with Stone.

Nothing is going to ruin this.

———

Stone is amazing. We go to the beach and wade along the shoreline with Trixie. As we walk hand in hand with my pup skipping along beside us, it's almost like we're a happy family. I can imagine our children walking with us, and I blush furiously as I peek a glance at Stone.

Is he thinking thoughts like that? He said he wanted to keep me, so I assume he wants me to be his girlfriend, but that doesn't mean he's considering marriage or anything like that yet.

I'm certainly not about to bring it up. I don't want to be one of those overly clingy girlfriends who pushes a guy for a commitment he's not ready for.

Still, I can't help thinking that Stone is it for me. He's *the one*. From the moment I saw him, I knew he was the one I wanted to give my virginity to, but I can also picture myself settling down with him, being with him and only him for the rest of my life.

Is this too soon, or am I just fuck-struck because he

gave me my first orgasm? Is this puppy love, or is it the real thing?

But as the days pass, something deep inside me tells me this is real, that what Stone and I have is a special gift. Call it intuition, but I feel it in my bones.

Now that we've shared our bodies, we're closer than ever. Now that we can touch each other freely, it seems like Stone's hands are always on me even when we're not making love. He holds my hand and wraps his arm around my shoulder when we're out walking. He touches my face and brushes my hair behind my ear when he kisses me. He takes every opportunity to touch me, and I love it, arching my body into his hands as shamelessly as my little slut of a dog.

Trixie is right there begging for attention, too. She and I are like bitches in heat fighting over the alpha male, but Stone is more than happy to give us all the attention we seek.

We spend nearly every moment together when Stone isn't hanging out with my brother. Jeremy and I haven't talked yet. I know that I'm going to have to face him soon, and it might be shitty of me, but I'm enjoying my newfound freedom with Stone.

While I'm not talking to my brother, I can't ignore the obstacle he presents between Stone and me. Stone sees Jeremy, but as soon as he gets home or when my brother leaves Stone's house, Stone is over at my house making love to me. Either that or we're going out for dinner or walks along the beach or boardwalk.

We're getting to know everything about one another, and we have more in common than I would have thought.

Even though Stone's parents were always around when they were alive, he knows what it's like to be without them. My parents are alive, but they've been absent my whole life. They've provided for my brother and me more than generously, but we never see them. Maybe once a year over FaceTime if we're lucky.

I sense the same yearning for a family within Stone. I understand his hesitance to tell my brother about us. Jeremy is like a brother to him, and I know how much it would crush him to lose his friendship.

If forced to choose between my brother or me, who would Stone choose? I don't want him to have to choose at all, so I hope my brother will get on board with our relationship—especially when he sees how much Stone and I mean to each other. I don't know about Stone, but I already know that I'm completely in love with him. Anything he asked me to do, I would do it.

Of course, I haven't said those three little words to him because I don't want to put pressure on him if he doesn't feel the same way, but they burn within my soul every time he looks at me, every time he touches me.

I know that I'm the one who proposed that Stone and I keep our relationship a secret for a while, but I only said that because I was desperate to say anything to get the man to kiss me and take my virginity.

Now that we're spending so much time together, I hate sneaking around like I'm his dirty little secret. Even if I'm not talking to my brother, I want it all out in the open. I don't want to feel like I'm doing something wrong by being with the man I love, and it's stressing me out, wondering who Stone will choose if put to the test.

I find out soon enough one day when we're walking along the boardwalk. Stone suddenly pulls away from me, dropping his arm from the small of my back. A moment later, I see why.

"Stone, my man!" my brother greets him before casting cautious eyes at me.

My stomach plummets when Stone jumps away from me because he doesn't want my brother to see us together.

"Mia," Jeremy greets me gently as if I'm a frightened doe that will run away as soon as I see him.

"Hi, Jeremy," I greet him cordially. I'm not mad at

him anymore, but I'm still a bit hurt by his reaction to me going to design school. Stone promised me he would talk to him, and he has, but I haven't been ready to speak to Jeremy myself yet.

"What are you doing out here together?" my brother asks me as his eyes flick between Stone and me curiously.

"Oh, I saw Mia walking along and offered to lend her some company," Stone tells my brother.

Jeremy nods his head approvingly. "Always looking out for my little sis. I appreciate it, bro."

My heart falls. Stone just lied to my brother about our relationship, and this could have been a perfect opportunity for him to come clean and tell him about us. I know I agreed to wait to tell my brother about us, but it hurts having Stone pull away like it's wrong to be seen with me.

The hopelessness of our situation comes crashing down on me all over again, especially when my brother asks Stone to hit up a club with him.

Stone shakes his head. "Not tonight, man. Maybe some other time."

"That's what you've said for the past two weeks," my brother grumbles. "What's up with you, man?"

Stone avoids my gaze, and my stomach falls. It suddenly hits me like a ton of bricks. I've been naive to think that this was going to work. Stone and I can never be together. It's never going to be okay with my brother, and the sooner we accept that, the better. This is going to be hard enough as it is.

But it's like a bandage, right? You have to rip it off, and the sooner, the better.

"Thanks for keeping me company, Stone, but I'm good now. I'm going to head home. You and Jeremy go hang out and do whatever guys do."

Stone's brows furrow, and his eyes hold a multitude of emotions I don't want to decipher.

"Hey, can we talk later, Mia?" Jeremy asks hopefully.

I nod my head at him. "Sure. I'd like that. Just call me tomorrow or something."

I see the relief wash over my brother's face and feel a prick of guilt. He's probably been in hell worrying about me all this time. I wouldn't talk to him because I wasn't ready to come back to the real world and face reality.

But now that it's crystal clear that Stone and I can never be together without jeopardizing his relationship with my brother, there's no reason for me to put off my talk with my brother any longer.

I can almost feel Stone's eyes burning into me as I turn and make my way home.

It was a nice fantasy while it lasted, but that's all it was—a fantasy. Maybe Stone knew that all along and was just playing for as long as possible. It's evident from his actions today that Stone would never choose me over my brother.

Part of me can't blame him, but another part of me is tremendously hurt and jealous.

I don't know what I'm going to do now because Stone will still be in my brother's life. How can I see him every day knowing he can't be mine?

I guess it's a good thing I'm planning to go to college soon. When I was entertaining thoughts of being with Stone, I was planning on taking online classes and living at home, but now I need to sign up for the in-person classes—anything to get me out of the house and away from the man I love but can never have.

Tears prick my eyes when I walk in the door and Trixie comes bounding up to me, looking behind me for Stone. My poor girl has gotten used to having him around. Moisture rushes to my eyes. It's not just me who's going to have a broken heart. Trixie will too.

I burst into tears, sobs wracking my body as I slide down my door and put my head in my hands in despair.

CHAPTER 8

Stone

MIA BROKE UP WITH ME. She never actually said the words, but ever since that day Jeremy caught us together on the beach, she hasn't answered my calls or opened the door to me—no matter how much I shout, begging her to let me in.

She's barely set foot outside the house, no doubt because I'm sitting on my porch staring over at her house like a maniac.

I can only assume Trixie is going to the bathroom on those little training pads because Mia knows she'll run over here to me as soon as she lets the dog out. Hell, I miss the little pup almost as much as I miss

Mia. She's like my dog too. We're a family—Mia, Trixie, and me—or I thought we were.

The moment I jumped away from Mia and made excuses to her brother, I knew I fucked up. It felt like a sleazy thing to do, and I'm still kicking myself in the ass.

I should have pulled her closer and told him what she meant to me. I'm sure that's why she refuses to talk to me. She thinks I chose her brother over her, but that couldn't be farther from the truth. Hell, I don't want to choose at all, but if I have to, I'll choose Mia. My woman. Always. Nothing compares to her.

I was so desperate to have a family that I put my relationship with Jeremy on a pedestal. Yeah, he's like a brother to me, but I can't let that stop me from creating my own family with Mia. Jeremy is more than welcome to be a part of it. I want him to be, but if he can't deal with Mia and me being together, so be it. I need Mia like I need air to breathe. I have to make her understand that somehow.

That's why I'm sitting on my porch again, staring at her house. She has to come out sooner or later. I know her mail has been piling up, and she'll have to check it soon to see if she's gotten any correspondence from that design school. I wasn't lying to her when I said her designs were good and I believed in her. I'm not a fashion guru, but her designs are outstanding, and I could see the passion in her eyes when she talked about them.

I hope she's got the ball rolling on all that. I want her to chase her dreams and do what makes her happy.

I told her I'd fund her first fashion line. I've got enough money to make all her dreams come true if she lets me.

I sit forward in my chair like a dog perking up its ears when I see her front door finally open.

I'm already standing as Mia steps out, ready to go over there and pour my heart on the ground for her, when a fluffy ball of cinnamon comes zooming around her, fast as lightning.

"Trixie!" Mia screams as the dog comes racing across the yard to me.

Just then, I hear the squealing of tires and look to my right to see a car skidding off the road to avoid hitting another car that swerved into its lane.

My eyes flick back over to the cinnamon-colored fur ball still racing toward me. I act without thinking and run over to meet the pup, grabbing her up in my arms as I roll us out of the path of the oncoming vehicle.

I hear Mia's screams over the screeching of tires as I land on my back with an oomph.

Trixie's wet little tongue licks all over my face, and I don't know if she's saying thank you for saving her from imminent danger or if she's just happy to see me. I would guess it's the latter since she seems nothing but overjoyed. I don't think she even realizes the danger she just put herself in.

Then next moment, Mia is bending over us, tears streaming down her face as she sobs. "Oh, my God. Are you two okay?" She runs one hand all over Trixie's fur while stroking my face frantically with the other, her eyes flicking over me, checking me for injury.

"Stone," she chokes out my name.

"I'm okay, sweetheart," I promise her. "And Trixie is fine too."

I work to soothe her. She's in hysterics, and for a good reason. The driver of the vehicle gets out to check on us, relieved to see everyone is okay. He apologizes profusely for swerving into my yard, but I assure him I understand and that no harm was done. He did what he thought he had to do to avoid a collision when the other driver swerved into his lane.

Mia is still crying, her eyes red-rimmed as she holds Trixie close. She nuzzles her face into the pup's fur as if she were her child. I understand the sentiment. Trixie is like our baby. I didn't even hesitate to put myself in harm's way for that little pup, and I'd do it all over again. My heart clenches at the thought of anything happening to Mia or Trixie.

It suddenly hits me what a great mother Mia would make.

Jeremy's voice breaks into my thoughts when I hear him calling out for his sister. A car door slams and he comes rushing over. Before he reaches us, I sit up and grab the back of Mia's neck, pulling her to me for a kiss. I'm conscious her brother is watching, so I keep it PG-13 as I stake my claim on his sister.

When I pull back, Mia looks at me with wide eyes.

"I love you, Mia. I've been dying to tell you that for days, but you wouldn't come out to see me."

Tears shimmer in her eyes. "I love you too, Stone. I'm sorry. So sorry. But I didn't want to come between you and my brother."

Jeremy is gawking down at us. "What the hell is all this?" He waves a hand between Mia and me.

I stand up and pull Mia next to me, wrapping my arm around her while she holds onto her little pup. Straightening my shoulders, I look my best friend in the eye and tell him the truth that's been burning in me for weeks. "I love your sister, Jeremy, and I intend to marry her. If she'll have me, that is." I look down at Mia.

Her eyes are shimmering with tears as she nods her head. "Oh, Stone. Yes! Yes, yes, I will marry you."

My heart feels lighter than it has in days at hearing Mia agree to be my wife.

Jeremy is still gawking at us, so I eye him warily, waiting for his reaction. His mouth works, but no words come out.

When he's finally able to speak, he asks, "How long has this been going on?"

I answer him truthfully. "I wanted Mia from the moment I first saw her. I knew she was the one, but then I found out she was your sister." I shake my head. "I didn't think you'd be cool with that, man, so we've been denying our feelings for each other because we didn't want to upset you."

I look at him cautiously, trying to gauge my best friend's reaction to this bombshell we've just dropped on him.

His eyes flick between us until they finally land on Mia. "Do you love him?"

Mia blushes as she looks up at me. "Yes, I do."

Jeremy turns his question to me. "You love my sister?"

I don't even hesitate. "With every fiber of my being."

There's a long moment of silence while Mia and I

stare into each other's eyes with Jeremy watching on. It's all out in the open now, and while I pray he accepts it, I'm not giving her up either way.

Jeremy finally clears his throat. "Well, when I said I wanted us to be a family, this isn't exactly what I meant." He gives me a wry smile. "Guess we're truly going to be bros then." He grins.

"Yeah," I exhale, and my shoulders relax. I'm relieved beyond measure that he's taking this all so well.

"You're going to have to do right by my baby sis, though," he tells me sternly. "Give her a proper wedding. I'll be the best man," he volunteers.

"Only if you agree not to take me to a strip club or something," I tell him seriously.

Jeremy looks at me with respect in his eyes. "You know it all makes sense now. Ever since you got into town, you weren't into going out with me. I have to say it pleases the hell out of me now that I know that the chick you've been digging on is my sister."

"So, you're okay with all of this?" Mia asks him cautiously.

Jeremy nods. "Yes, Mia. You were right. You're not a little kid anymore, but you'll always be my baby sis. I'm okay with this because I know Stone. I know he's a great man, and you'll be in good hands with him. I wouldn't trust my sister to anyone else," he tells me with a rare hint of emotion in his eyes.

We don't say anything else, but the look that passes between us communicates everything we need to say. He knows I'll do right by Mia.

Jeremy makes everything lighthearted again when he jokes dryly, "Back when I told you to make sure guys kept their paws off her, I suppose I should have specified that went for you too."

I glance down at Mia and place a kiss on her head. "Yeah, there was no way that was going to happen. I tried. I really did, but she's just so—"

Jeremy holds up his hand and makes a face. "I don't need to know all the details, man. In fact, I'm going to head off and leave you two lovebirds alone."

"See you later, man," I call after him as he heads back to his car to give us space.

"So, you couldn't keep your paws off me, huh?" Mia looks up at me teasingly with Trixie in her arms.

"You already know I couldn't," I tell her as I bend to place a kiss on her lips.

A little tongue snakes out to get in between our lips.

"Trixie, ew!" Mia giggles and pushes the little dog's head down while I chuckle. "You jealous little slut," she reprimands her.

I cock an eyebrow at her.

"What?" Mia teases me. 'She is! She's been a shameless slut for you since you moved in next door. All we've done is fight over you from the moment we saw you carrying those heavy boxes into your house."

I laugh at the image Mia paints of her and her little pup in competition for my affections.

"There's plenty of room in my heart for both of my girls," I assure them both as I stroke my hand over Trixie's fur and kiss Mia's sweet lips.

My girls.

My family.

Four Years Later

Stone

I PLACE my hand on my wife's pregnant belly. Trixie is sleeping in her lap, curled up against her protectively. I swear the pup knows that Mia is pregnant because she loves to sleep near her stomach, almost as if she's protecting our unborn child.

It's adorable.

My girls.

We already know the baby is a girl. Mia couldn't wait to find out so she could begin designing clothes for our little one. She's graduated from design school, and we waited until after she was done with her studies before she let me put a baby inside her.

The moment she walked off the stage with her diploma, I pulled her into the car and got her good and bred. All I fantasized about when she was in school was getting her pregnant and starting our family. I threw those motherfucking birth control pills out the window the day she graduated.

Mia's in the process of launching her first fashion line now, and I couldn't be prouder.

While she designs all day, I run my software business. We both work from home, and we love it that way because we can spend as much time with each other as we want—and our little Trixie.

Our houses are still next door to one another. Sometimes we stay in mine. Sometimes we stay in hers. Maybe we don't need two houses, but we're reluctant to sell either one.

We don't want anyone moving in next door to us, so we're keeping both the properties. Maybe when our little one grows up, she'll want to live next to her mom and dad.

Mia places her hand atop mine and looks up at me with a smile.

I tuck her hair back behind her ear as we sit on the

beach, watching as the sun sets over the Pacific Ocean. It's one of our favorite things to do.

I stroke my hand over the sleeping dog's fur. Trixie doesn't stir other than to arch her head slightly up into my hand, her eyes still closed.

After that little fiasco with her almost getting hurt, Mia and I decided that she needed some sort of training. While we didn't put her through a grueling obedience school, we watched some videos together on how to train your pup, and we worked with her until she listened to our commands.

She's still a free spirit, but she's a lot more well-behaved and doesn't run out the door every time you open it.

And it may have been unconventional, but when we got married, Trixie was right there in Mia's arms as we said our vows and I kissed the bride.

The little pup wasn't going to have it any other way.

We tried making her sit beside our feet, but she kept jumping on Mia's dress, insisting on being picked up. She wanted to make sure that she was a part of the ceremony.

And while Jeremy was my best man, he was also the one to walk Mia down the aisle.

Her parents didn't even bother to fly in for the wedding.

Oh, well. Mia insists that she didn't miss anything because she doesn't know her parents that well anyway. She says that Jeremy, Trixie, and I are all the family she needs, and I agree.

I scoot to sit behind Mia and pull her back against my chest, wrapping my arms around her. She leans her head against my shoulder as we watch the sun go down together.

We don't speak. We're comfortable enough with one another that we don't need words. We soak up each other's presence, our bodies molded together.

When the sun has completely set and only the moon shimmers over the waves, I glance around to check we're alone on the beach.

This is the moment I've been waiting for.

I lift Mia into my lap and sit Trixie on the sand beside us, where she walks in a little circle before laying down and immediately going back to sleep.

I'm already completely hard in anticipation of making love to my wife here on the beach in the moonlight. I push Mia's hair to the side so I can place a tender kiss against the smooth column of her throat. She moans as I continue to worship her neck.

I pull my cock out before I pull her little bikini

bottoms discreetly to the side as I push gently up into her. I wrap an arm around Mia's waist. Her little hands clutch onto it as I push myself completely inside her, placing a kiss behind her ear.

Christ, she's still as tight as the day I first took her.

She moans, her neck falling to the side to allow me greater access to the smooth column of her flesh. "Stone," she whispers my name.

"You feel so good, baby," I murmur as I begin to move slowly within her.

She's not very far along, but I've been taking her with more care than usual since I found out she's pregnant. I don't want to do anything to put her or this baby at risk.

She pushes down onto me as I thrust into her, our bodies rocking slowly until our release crashes over us in gentle, rolling waves like those breaking on the shoreline.

Mia's muscles clench around me as I spill into her with a shudder. I wrap my arms around her and hold her tightly against my chest, burying my face in the nape of her neck.

"I love you, wife," I tell her.

I hear the smile in her voice as she says, "I love you too, husband."

I've never been more content.

I have my girls, my family, and that's all I'll ever need.

THE END

Visit Emma's website to get a FREE book you can't get anywhere else: www.authoremmabray.com.